KAY THOMPSON'S

ELOISE IN

PARIS

DRAWINGS BY
HILARY KNIGHT

SIMON AND SCHUSTER

One teatime this telephone was ringing its head off

so I picked it up

and oh my Lord it was the front desk saying

Eloise there's a telegram down here for you

do you want us to send it up?

And I said well by all means send it up right away

pronto at once on the double zibbity zap clink clank

hang up that phone

and skibble out of that door

Nanny is rawther long-sighted

It was a telegram from my mother

Oh my Lord we are going to Paris France
to get roses in our cheeks

If you are going to Paris France
you have to turn into French and absolutely go wild
and put adhesive tape on you
and fall down a lot and sklathe the window
and stretch into the curtain and grab Nanny's ankle
and be dragged around

Then you have to get on that telephone
and tell everyone that you're going

Hello Room Service
this is me ELOISE
we're going to Paris France goodbye

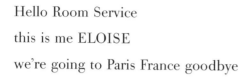

Hello give me the Porter please
will you bring our trunks to the top floor
yes we're going to Paris France France

Hello give me the Bell Captain please
will you kindly send up some twine
we want to wrap up our trunk
we're going to Paris France
bon voyage and thanks a lot

Hello get me the Housekeeper please
goodbye goodbye goodbye

Hello get me the General Manager's office
s'il vous plaît
Hello Mr Voit this is Me ELOISE
kindly forward our post to Paris France
we're leaving tout de suite which is right away
bon voyage and merci beaucoup

Then Nanny had to go and call
Dr Hadley to get our injections

While he is taking off his coat
you have to fall down on the bed
and hide and count the pillows for a while with your head under it
and pull everything on top of you and glue your eyes
and be stiffer and stiffer and sort of
disguise your arm under the quilt and then slowly sklathe it
out about an inch or so and zambo sting sting stinger

Then you have to have your head bandaged
with cold compresses
and hit Dr Hadley with the flyswatter
and clink clank pick up that phone
and call Room Service
to send up four peach melba and
three straight Johnny Walker Black
without ice and charge it please
merci beaucoup

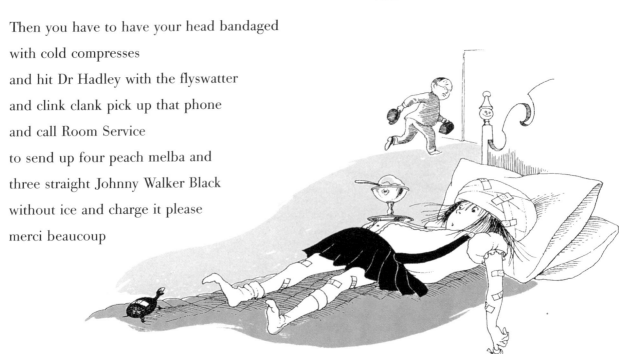

Dr Hadley went to Harvard
and always wears a derby except when he's operating

Clink clank pick up that phone
and call the Irving Trust Co.
to get those passports over here right away at once

And you should see our passport pictures

Here's the thing of it
I am rawther photogenic

And oh my Lord did we ever have to pack pack pack

Here's what you have to take if you're going to Paris France
Mary Jane button hook
Pliers
Consommé container
Hotel kit

Here's what else you have to take
Everything

I always pack my parachute
and
I always wear my foreign identification travel tag
whenever I go to Paris
which is a picture of me on one side
and a mirror on the other
for me to see who I am if I need to

I am usually me ELOISE

At the very last minute Emily came over
from Central Park to say goodbye
She is allergic to the humidity
and suffers quite a bit
I left the bawthroom window open for her
so that she could come in and enjoy the
air conditioning while we were away
and said à bientôt Emily dear
which is see you later

Then get out in that Hall
and close that door
and put on that Do Not Disturb sign
just in case

When that lift comes up
you have to be ready to
get in get in get in
and will you get in for Lord's sake

We had 37 pieces of luggage
including these 2 wire hangers this camera these 2 bottle tops
the hot-water bottle and 2 cans of kippers from Gristede's

And will you get out get out get out
for Lord's sake

I always travel incognito

Weenie said goodbye
to the Doorman
and thanks a lot

I always say au revoir
to the Plaza whenever
I go to Paris France

Everyone knew we were going but no one cried

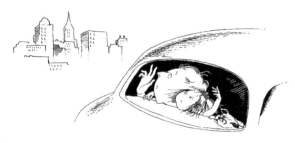

We took a taxi to the airport
It's the best way by far by far by far
Nanny says it's more romantic
Oooooooooooooooo I absolutely love Nanny

When you get there
you have to check your ticket
to see if you're going
and buy a mint or so

And oh my Lord
there was this enormously large plane
and these motors were granning and turning themselves around
and there were all these men running around
and this petrol was there
and we had to walk up all these steps and get into it

Sabena is the only airline
that will allow you to travel with a turtle

The absolutely first thing you have to do
is put on your lifebelt
and go and see what's up

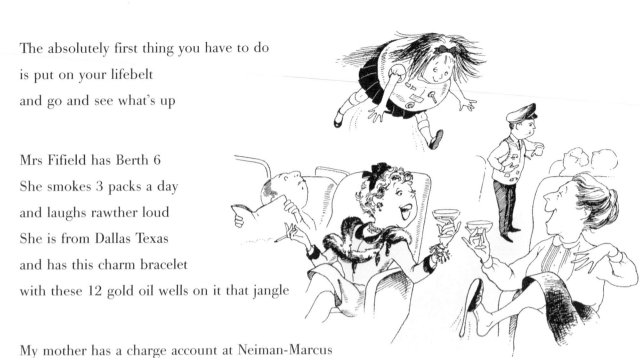

Mrs Fifield has Berth 6
She smokes 3 packs a day
and laughs rawther loud
She is from Dallas Texas
and has this charm bracelet
with these 12 gold oil wells on it that jangle

My mother has a charge account at Neiman-Marcus

Actually the pilot has nothing to do
so you can help him count the comets

I didn't have my nap today
but Nanny says pas de quoi
because New York is 6 hours behind us

During the night
the motors are on fire
Absolutely no one slept

It was raining when we landed in Brussels
but we didn't get our feet wet
We walked right up into the air into this darling little helicoptaire

When you get to the French border
you have to begin to parler français

Weenie's favourite word is d'accord
which is OK

Skipperdee's favourite word is zut
which is oh hecko

Nanny's favourite is regardez
which is look look look

My favourite word is pas de quoi
which is
oh it's quite all right I'm sure that you didn't mean
to crush my hand in the door even though it is bleeding and
practically throbbing with pain it's quite all right it doesn't
matter

no is mais non
yes is mais oui
vous êtes you
je suis Me ELOISE

Then Nanny said
ooh ooh ooh regardez
and there was Paris France

You have to show your passport
in case you are these smugglers
who have just escaped
without a quota

I always tie my bottle caps around my chest and conceal these grape
seeds
inside of this Band-Aid and push it down into the left side of my leg
into the lower part of my sock near the ankle bone on the inside
and hide my bubble gum where they absolutely never discover it

Then we went through this door
and there was Koki
with a telegram from my mother
He is my mother's lawyer's chauffeur
and speaks several languages
Nanny says that's jolly dee
because if she has to cope she prefers
to do it in English

He gave me this Paris bouquet and said
Allo Chérie
and I said
Allo Chéri

Oh my Lord
it was my absolutely first conversation on French soil

Koki is 27 and has hair that hurts your hand
and does absolutely nothing but smile
He weighs 137 without his crest ring
and hibernates in the winter
in the south of France
Here's what Koki says all the time
ditto
Here's what he likes
raspberry tartes
ditto cowboy movies
Here's what he hates
motorcycles
ditto bicycles
Here's what I like
Paris
ditto Koki

And oh my Lord we had 38 pieces of luggage
including the camera the 2 wire hangers the hot-water bottle
and the 2 cans of kippers
and somebody's briefcase with SN on it that didn't even belong to us
Pas de quoi d'accord and zut

I actually prefer the Renault Dauphine whenever I am in Paris France

We sang all the way in

Fro-mage is cheese n' fish is pois-son n' boats is les bat-eaux

n' trees is arbres 'n flowers is fleurs n' hor-ses is chev-aux oh!

Brid-ges is ponts n' streets is rues n' church-es is e-glises

And who is we in Par-is if you please? Who? We'se Nan-ny n' Wee-nie n' Skip-per-dee and Me E-LO-ISE

Koki shouted bravo and applauded quite a bit

and turned right on the Pont St-Michel

Here's what they have a lot of in Paris

pigeons

There are several hotels in Paris

We prefer the Relais Bisson
on the Quai des Grands Augustins
because of the sea breeze
and the salt air from the Seine

The lobby is rawther petite

and Mme and M. Dupuis are absolutely French

Mme Dupuis smiled a lot and said ah Nahnee bonjour bonjour

and Nahnee said ah bonjour bonjour bonjour Mme Dupuis

and oh my Lord M. Dupuis kissed Nahnee's hand

And Mme Dupuis said ah bonjour Mademoiselle es-tu un enfant terrible?

and I looked up at her and repondu

which is replied

no merci Mme Dupuis je suis Me ELOISE

I always use the French politesse

which is be polite

if you possibly can

There is no Bell Captain

so you can imagine

There is no lift

Pas de quoi
Here's what you have to do
Mind the stairs

When you are in your chambre which is your room
you are allowed to fall on the bed and sort of sklathe
yourself into these large pillows for a while
because here's what you are
absolutely fatiguée
which is tired tired tired

The absolutely first thing you have to do
is put on your bedroom slippers
which is pantoufles

Then if you decide that you'd like to have
a little iced lemonade or something like that
to cool you off with fresh mint in it
clink clank pick up that telephone
and while you are waiting
for someone to answer

you can yawn several times
and unpack and go and see what's up

The water is French

Skipperdee has his own private swimming pool

Nahnee says you have to hide everything because
if you don't
oh my Lord the police will be involved
and will come and blow their whistles

Nahnee hid our money in a secret hiding place
but we never found it
she forgot where she put put put it

M. Delacroix lives next door
and his daughter is in Bombay
and went swimming with her brother-in-law
who swallowed this peach seed

M. Delacroix gets quite a few postal cards

And then whack
you hear all this whacking and ne quittez pas and zuk zuk zuk zwhocky zuk zuk swgock
zuk zukky zuk zuk zwock nnnnnnnnnnnnnnnnnnnnnnnnnnnnnnnnnnnnnnnnnn
and you are disconnected

Here's the thing of it
Clink clank hang up that phone
and simply send a telegram

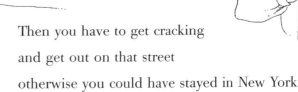

Then you have to get cracking
and get out on that street
otherwise you could have stayed in New York

So the first thing you have to do
is put on your gloves

and zap into the foyer

and send a telegram or so

You absolutely cannot go anywhere in Paris without your map

Oh my Lord

il y a beaucoup de traffic in Paris

and that's a lot

I usually skibble along the quai for a walk
which is promenade

There is also
beaucoup de this

and beaucoup de that

LE PIGEON

PONT NEUF

beaucoup de dog

beacoup de cat

FOUJITA
GALERIE
PAUL PETRIDES

Beaucoup de these

beaucoup de those

Il y a beaucoup de quelque chose
which is something
Oooooooooo I absolutely love quelque chose

Paris is a place where you have to be to see it
so you have to take your British sit-down stick
and la regardez

French bread makes very good skis

You can go across the Seine by land or by sea
We prefer the sea voyage
Nahnee is always Lord Nelson
I am usually Me ELOISE

Il y a beaucoup de fish

You absolutely have to have your camera ready at all times
in case something comes in front of you and is in focus so that you can
take a picture of everything even if you don't see it

For instance
if you want to take a
picture of this statue
or this friend or this
balloon in a hurry or
something like that

take that camera and
press it against your
forehead and turn this
knob at the bottom to
the right until it hits
this blue mark underneath
the red

then press it against
your forehead until
they all say blue and
sling it over your
shoulder and scratch
your ankle perhaps on
the inside and squint

You can have them
developed right away

If you want to
you can take the case off

Sometimes they turn out

I am all over the Etoile

Sometimes I go on on a bicycle

but not without a horn

If you want to
simply walk across
they will stop for you

And

oh my Lord

there was this most terriblest crise which is crisis

I think I got a very good picture of it

And

is there everly a lot of promenading on the Avenue des Champs-Elysées

and those cars come up on the pavement and purr behind you

Here's what you have to do in Paris

keep moving a lot

like looking up

or sitting down in a pavement café

I am toujours which is always at Fouquet's

I usually sit in the front row
I can see better there
and have a tarte mirabelle or so

You cawn't cawn't cawn't get a good cup of tea
they simply do not boil the water
so you have to have champagne
with a peach in it instead

We ran into Mrs Fifield
She was absolutely breathing
and had spent all of her
Traveller's Cheques at Pierre Balmain
on the Rue François 1ᵉʳ
She speaks no French
so you can imagine

Les pigeons at Fouquet's are rawther healthy
but not one French pigeon is as fat as Emily
You have to speak to them in French
because here's what they are
français
and you simply have to tell them
to
quittez quittez quittez
which is go away Chéri
or they will sit on your head and
knock your glasses off

I usually give them a slight squirt
with this soda siphon
to cool them off in this hot sun
so they don't get overheated
and waddle themselves over or so
It is rawther refreshing for them

Some of their feet are pink
and their eyes are red
but they don't cough

I took this picture of this pigeon
talking to this soda siphon
C'est bon

Here's what I have to do every French morning
sklathe myself out of bed
and wave to the fishermen
and say bonjour Notre Dame

Then I have to brush my hair
until it bounces

put milk of cucumber
on my face in layers

and look in the mirror
for a sec or so
and je m'amuse

and yawn for a while
or smell the peonies
or something like that

Then I do my
champagne exercises

Weenie is bubble keeper

We toujours have café au lait

which is petit déjeuner

and a croissant which is absolutely delicious

Weenie took a bawth in Perrier water

and it tingled him with these needles and got up his nose

It was rawther refreshing for him

Skipperdee swims most of the time

He prefers the Australian crawl

Weenie sleeps a lot under the bed

with his bones en gelée where it's cooler

He is absolutely gaining weight

ditto Skipperdee

ditto Nahnee

ditto Me ELOISE

Here's what gives Nahnee a mal de tête which is a headache

pigeons

So far I have 18 champagne corks

Every French night I take a footbawth with this little petite of lettuce soap

ditto eau-de-Cologne

ditto milk of cucumber

Lean out of the window and say bon soir to Notre Dame

and hit the hot-water bottle

Then I have to put my shoes out
in the hall to be dusted
because the French cobblestones
turn them into absolute scuff
but be sure to put your name flags
on all of them
or M. Delacroix will be wearing
your pantoufles in the morning

I usually have a bottle of Perrier water
and je me repose
which is rest myself
and read the Herald Tribune for a while

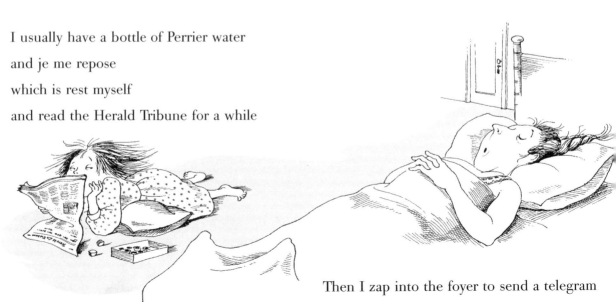

Then I zap into the foyer to send a telegram

The concierge reads it out loud just in case

MEESTER GENE AH VOIT   RESIDENT MANAGAIR

OTEL PLAZA FEEFTY-NINTH STREET NEW YORK USA

DEAR MEESTAIR AH VOIT YOU KNOW THAT AH SWEETCH AH

WHEECH CONNECTS AH THE AIR CONDEESIONING ON THE AH EIGHTH

AH FLOOR? I AH DON'T THEENK EET'S AH WORKEEENG AH HERE'S

WHERE AH ZE PLOOG EEZ EEN PAREE WEEZ ME   ELOISE

Then I roam around the stairs

for several hours or so

not knowing what I am doing

M. Delacroix gets his shoes from Macy's
Some people's feet are rawther large

Bonne nuit
is good night

Il y a beaucoup de sights to see
For instance you can go to the Eiffel Tower
It is absolutely large and rawther high
so I always tie my binoculaires
to my head in this breeze
and go up sideways

Nahnee hid her money in her stocking

ATTENTION
AUX
PICKPOCKETS

GLACES

Très is very
Agréable is absolutely pleasant
An ice-cream wagon is très agréable

I took this picture of Weenie talking
to this French snail
It is rawther fluzzery

I toujours take my parapluie

which is umbrella

to the Madeleine

and have some almonds in a noisy sack

Paris raindrops are larger

Or you can go to the Sacré-Coeur

for gas balloons

Or to the British Embassy

They boil the water there

Or you can go to l'Escargot

Everyone was having a snail

I had potage du jour

There are several

restaurants in Paris

Langoustines make very good fingernails

Paris is the world of fish

Or you can go to the races
I always sit in the front row
and watch these horses come running around with these tails
and they have these veins sticking out
and they are snorting
and rolling their eyes

Some of them win

Or you can go to the Ritz
in this carriage and this horse
which is right behind Napoleon
and have tea in the garden
with a green napkin and this gravel

Or you can go to the zoo
for this rawther French safari

Or to the ballet at the Opéra

I took a royal jelly gumdrop cigar
and captured these three gnats
who kept hanging around

72915

Or you can go to the Flea Market
Voici what they have there

this red feather fan
or this fur piece
or this wedding dress
or these elephant tusks
if you need something like that
and quite a lot of other rawther valuable things

I got two champagne corks
and had them shipped back to the United States
They were rawther a bargain

Paris is the world of fashion

Or you can go to the movies

We have been to 37 movies and have seen Orson Welles 19 times

Or you can do a little petite of shopping
There are absolutely nothing but streets in Paris

Here's what you have to do
point at everything and say

oooooooooooo regardez this

and

oooooooooooo regardez this

I usually have to touch everything

and sort of pick it up

and feel it quite a bit

Sometimes here's what you have to say
Pardonnez-moi Chérie my dear
but je suis a little petite fatiguée

I always take a plunge in the fountains
whenever I am in Paris
It is rawther refreshing

Il fait chaud is
it is hot
n'est-ce pas is
is it not?

Nahnee took this absolutely darling picture of me

If there is a lot of rain and wet
simply go to the Louvre

Mrs Fifield was behind the Venus de Milo
so you can imagine

Here's what you have to do
tippy around on the parquet floor
and hold your neck up with this guide

There are several paintings or so

And oh my Lord on the way out
there was this most terriblest crise

There were these two attendants there and this woman in this sweataire
and they would not give us our camera
or Weenie or Skipperdee or our parapluie
because they said we had to have this ticket
so we said well nous avons perdu
which is we have lost our ticket
and they said
pas de ticket pas de camera
pas de tortue pas de chien pas de parapluie

and oh my Lord
they made some of us go all the way back up those stairs
and get it where some of us had left it behind
the Winged Victory of Samothrace

Here's what Nahnee says
Ah! the French the French the French
Here's what I say
Pas de quoi d'accord and zut

I toujours tweak the Apollo Belvedere
whenever I leave the Louvre

I always go barefoot to St-Germain-des-Prés for a salade niçoise

Koki took this absolutely darling picture of us

A melon makes a very good iced foot bucket

and a very good heat-ray hat

Skipperdee kissed Weenie quite a bit

M. Dior designed a dress for me

and it is absolutely chic

although I would have preferred a tassel or two

Pas de quoi

Here's what I am

a clothes horse which is cheval

One Sunday which is dimanche

Koki came by in the little petite Dauphine and said Allo Chérie where to

which is où

and I said

simply drive me to some palace Koki dear

He is my best friend in all of Paris

All you need to know about Versailles is that Louis XIV

was the father of Louis XV and Louis XVI lived at the Louvre

I think

Il y a beaucoup de cobblestones in Paris

and some of our feet

are getting round

The Hall of Mirrors is an unusual room

I saw absolutely nothing else but Me ELOISE

It was très agréable

There are absolutely no kings in France

Koki took this absolutely darling picture of me eating gâteau
which is cake

I never go to the Bois de Boulogne
without my French sweataire
because there might be a picnic

They had this little lake
which is a lac
and I ran into this French duck
It was très agréable

We played mumbly-peg
and counted the clovers

French sandwiches are absolument large
and we had to put all these flags on them
so we could tell which one was anchovy
and which one was concombres
which is cucumbers
and which one was grass

There are quite a few people who are not even looking at each other

Koki played the guitar and I danced the arabesque

while he sang this French chanson about Les Passions des Etoiles

which is about this girl who lost her shoe in this forest

There are very few places where you cannot take a chien

The Paris sun will burn your arm if you are fishing in it

and you will have to get calcimine lotion and spread it on in layers

so a good time to go fishing is in the evening

which is soir

or if you want to you can go in the rain

which is pluie

You have to be content with everything in France

for instance if you want a jelly bean

you can have almond paste instead

or if you want the sun you can have pluie

Oh I absolutely miss the Plaza

ditto Room Service

ditto the Bell Captain

Oh my Lord c'est difficile when you are a child

which is difficult

Froid is right

Chaud is left

and you can count on it

practically all of the time

but not always

Here's what you have to watch out for in Paris

prickly heat on your stomach

We usually dress for dinner

On my last night in Paris
I always wear my pink pantoufles to Maxim's
and say bon soir Albert
he is French

He admired my necklace
of champagne corks

They have this music which is la musique
which is playing its head off
It is rawther festive

You have to regardez le menu for quite a while
It is rawther fluzzery

Mrs Fifield had soufflé
We had these darling little strawberries
which are absolutely wild

Here's what you can do while you're waiting
look around a lot
or you can play with your face a little

When you get l'addition which is the bill
la regardez for a little petite and simply say
la chargez s'il vous plaît Albert and merci
My mother knows Maxim

I absolutely did not want to leave because
j'aime beaucoup Paris

I sent the baggage down early

Mrs Fifield called to ask what plane we were taking
She had Berth 6

I gave Koki all of my photographs
so that he would never forget
our trip to Paris
He gave me
this champagne cork
from the south of France
and I said
Oooooooooooooo je vous aime beaucoup
which is
I absolutely love you Koki

Here's how many postal cards I've sent
67 airmail
which is par avion

We were slightly overweight
especially Weenie

Nahnee said à bientôt Koki
and merci merci merci
Koki said
au revoir Chérie
and I said
au revoir Chéri
It was rawther sad
which is triste triste triste

When we got to New York

oh my Lord

we had 114 pieces of luggage

but we could not find the briefcase

it was perdu which is lost

We had absolutely nothing to declare

You can hide your bottle caps behind your knee caps

nobody looks there on a child

Absolutely nothing had been done while I was away

Mr Voit is partially French

Express to the top floor please

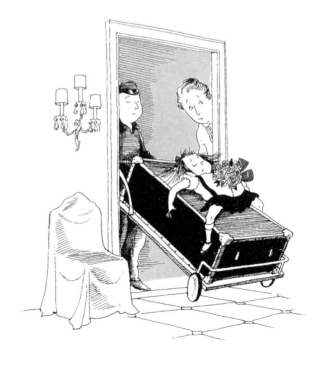

Clink clank pick up that phone and call Room Service
They were very glad to hear my voice
and said yes Eloise
and I said

Allo Room Service
C'est moi ELOISE
Kindly send up 4 watermelon on the rocks
ditto 4 champagnes
ditto 1 sodawater please
to the top floor s'il vous plaît
and le chargez merci beaucoup

Ooooooooooooooooo I absolutely love the Plaza
Clink clank hang up that phone and je me repose

Then Nanny said
Eloise I wonder if you could tell me
who who who left the bawthroom window open
while we were away
do you know who that could possibly be?
and I said well
actuellement Nahnee dear je ne sais pas
and then Nanny said
well do you think it might have been you Chérie?
and I said oh my Lord Nahnee dear
c'est difficile to say
Mais pourquoi do you ask
Nahnee dear s'il vous plaît?
Then Nanny sklathed herself over
to this bawthroom door
and opened it up zap
and said regardez

regardez   regardez

my Lord

Il y a beaucoup de pigeons in our bawthroom

Emily and her friends were very glad to see us

J'aime beaucoup le Plaza which is

Ooooooooooooo I absolutely love the Plaza

Now about that post box

SIMON AND SCHUSTER
First published in Great Britain in 2001 by Simon & Schuster UK Ltd
Africa House, 64-78 Kingsway, London WC2B 6AH

This paperback edition first published in 2006

Originally published in 1957 by Simon & Schuster, New York

A CIP catalogue record for this book is available from the British Library upon request

EAN 9781416916598

ISBN 1-416-91659-8

Printed in Italy

1 3 5 7 9 10 8 6 4 2